The Skin Spinners

ALSO BY JOAN AIKEN

Midnight Is a Place

The Mooncusser's Daughter
A PLAY FOR CHILDREN

Street
A PLAY

JOAN AIKEN

The Skin Spinners
POEMS

Drawings by Ken Rinciari

THE VIKING PRESS   NEW YORK

ACKNOWLEDGMENTS

Grateful acknowledgment is made to the following for permission
to use previously published material. "Nate's Song" from
Nightbirds on Nantucket, copyright © 1966 by Joan Aiken;
"John's Song" from *Not What You Expected*, copyright ©
1974 by Joan Aiken. Reprinted by permission of Doubleday &
Company, Inc. and Jonathan Cape Limited. "Rhyme for Night"
from *Winterthing* by Joan Aiken. Copyright © 1972 by Joan
Aiken. Reprinted by permission of Holt, Rinehart and Winston,
Publishers, and Jonathan Cape Limited.

"The Ballad of Newington Green" has appeared in *Puffin Post*,
"Cat," "Do It Yourself," and "Fable" in *Cricket*; "Grandfather"
and "The Smile" in *The Horn Book*; "Mice" in the *Wychwood
School Magazine*; "Palace Cook's Tale" in *Puffin Annual*; and
"Socks for the Sirens" in Argosy (England).

For John and Jane
J.A.

For skin-deepers and deep-skinners
and Adria, I draw the line
K.R.

Contents

MYSTERIOUS THINGS

LEGENDS

PEOPLE

BALLADS

Simple Things

DO IT YOURSELF

Buy our little magazine
Quite the smallest ever seen
Printed on a square of tissue
Just
One
Letter
In
Each
Issue.
With each issue, given free
A seed pearl and a pinch of tea.

Thread the seed pearl, save the pinch
Make a necklace, inch by inch,
Fill a warehouse, ton by ton,
Save the letters, one by one,
Lay
The
Letters
In
A
Row
Make the rhyme you're reading now

SNAIL

Snail's never had to hitchhike yet:
He moves inside his maisonnette
He has no need for truck or trailer
Snail lives in jail, but snail's the jailer.

Pity him not, for, truth to tell
He's happy in his clammy cell
He has no need for shoes or socks
His lunch is leaves of hollyhocks
He has no need for road or rail
His house is made of fingernail
And in this stately pleasure dome
He travels, yet remains at home.

At night, calm, cautious Snail is used
To roam, while rooks and robins roost
He greets the coming of the dawn
By winding in his shining horn;
Composed, within his gliding grotto,
"A bird in the hand" is *not* his motto.

PLANE THINKING

*For my father, who challenged me to write a sonnet using
the line "airplane or aeroplane, or just plain plane."*

Thoughts like slow fish move upward, while the plane
(Airplane or aeroplane or just plain jet)
Bores eastward into dark, and into wet,
Then, like wise fish, nimbly escape again,
Sink from the surface, needle through the net
And thus resume their submarine terrain.

(Thoughts like blind fish, unable to sustain
Air's lack of pressure, reason's alphabet?)

Meanwhile the steady Boeing, ploughing slow
Through air in boulders, air in breakers, air
Streaming from wings like fog, like smoke, like snow
This plane, this representative from care,
Takes us, dumb freight, who do not wish to go,
Continuum-packed, the label reading: *Where?*

GUIDE TO LONDON

In Love Lane, in Thistle Grove
Beware the thorny treasure-trove

In Bread Street, in Friday Street
Useless to knock and ask for meat.

In Gun Street, in Powder Court,
Avoid misfeasance, fray, and tort.

In Hosier Lane, in Giltspur Street
Customers walk with jaunty feet.

In Pine Street, Paper Street, Sea Coal Lane
Kindle a fire and come out of the rain.

By Redberry Grove and Strawberry Hill
You may pick all day till the birds fall still.

In Daffodil Lane and Cuckoo Dene
London spring is fit for a queen.

But when you arrive at Turn Again Lane
If you want any more you must read it again.

RHYME FOR NIGHT

Dark is soft, like fur
Velvet, like a purr;
Lies warm, lies close
On fingers and toes

If dark cost much money
Rich men only
Would be able to pay
And rest them from day

If dark were not given
Each night from heaven
On field and town and park
Men would have to make dark

Dark is so warm, so deep
Without dark, how could we sleep?

BRIDGE

Here on the river's verge he stood
Scratching his forehead, at a loss
Our prehistoric ancestor
Wondering how to get across

His grandson's grandson found a way
Our grandsire's grandpa made a plan
Fetched stones and friends and logs and tools
And bridged the river, span by span

There is no other word for bridge
No other word would really do
To name a thing so simple and
So beautiful and useful too.

See how it curves from shore to shore
So many curves, all interblended
Bears traffic gamely on its back
For which it never was intended

Takes child to parent, friend to friend
Sweetheart to sweetheart, all dry-shod
And ghost to ghost, for all we know,
And god to man, and man to god.

To smash a bridge, among all crimes
Of vandalism is the worst
This bridge has stood five hundred years
Who breaks it, let him be accurst.

There is no other word for bridge
No other word would really do
To name a thing so simple and
So beautiful and useful too.

HAND OVER

It would be funny
if we didn't have money
How would we work out price?

One cat is better than twenty mice.
How would we tot up cost?
A vacuum cleaner is worth a ton of dust.
How to assess value?
A dozen sparrows equal one curlew.
How decide worth?
One rose to an acre of earth.
How figure expense?
A mad bull is worth a strong fence.
How fix a reasonable charge?
A good poem is worth a bit of bread and marge.

What would we call cheap?
A hurricane for a night's sleep.
And dear?
A lump of coal for a miner's fear.

MICE

I dropped a pea in the larder
swift in the cool wet dark
I heard it land on the sweating bricks
and roll to a corner. Hark!
what noise was that by the egg-vat?
(the shapes of great dishes loom
like ghosts in earthenware waiting
hid in the silent room).
A mouse stirred loud by the egg-vat
the slow eggs clicked and rolled
I put my hand among them
and felt one, stony cold.
I drew an egg out, dripping
and put my plate on the floor
it rang, like a fork on a glass bowl,
as I stepped back towards the door.
I felt in the dark for a mousetrap
and pushed it beside the peas
my feet were cold on the icy bricks
the cobwebs brushed my knees.
I lifted the latch and pulled it,
the waterglass egg gleamed white
(I dropped a pea in the larder)
I stepped out into the light.

HOUSE ON CAPE COD

Sharp sting of sand, saltwater stain
the house forgets, its boards retain
the wind sandpapered this demesne

old beams record the lash of rain
mimicked in timber's grey and grain
sharp sting of sand, saltwater stain.

Wind, storm, gale, tempest, hurricane
old timbers shrug and take the strain
the wind sandpapered this demesne

curtained by fog, sea's weathervane
drowse, house, awhile, dream, feel again
sharp sting of sand, saltwater stain

put on green grapevine's summerskein
creeper's crisscross on saltblurred pane
the wind sandpapered this demesne

hold, too, with love, man's wax-and-wane
his suffering heart, his shaping brain—
sharp sting of sand, saltwater stain
the wind sandpapered this demesne

ALGEBRA

A and one and two and B
Like fruit upon a drooping tree
swung in an elliptic curve
carry news along the nerve
four and potent five combine
to make the triply woven vine
that bears the complex product: nine.
> (And yet contrast this ninefold fruit
> Against the squareness of its root
> Buried beneath the noble tree
> Remains the humble taproot, three.)

PROVERBS

One of the things you never see:
an elephant's nest in a rhubarb tree

Leeks in Lent and garlic in May
these ought to keep the doctor away

When you're proposing to swim the Nile
don't make fun of the crocodile

Yolk of yellow in a whirl of white
daisy, day's eye, turns to the light

Thatch the river with pancakes when
mice are ready to trust in men

CAT

Old Mog comes in and sits on the newspaper
Old fat sociable cat
Thinks when we stroke him he's doing us a favour
Maybe he's right, at that.

A SHORT DIRECTORY
OF KENT

The people at Hayes
   Go their ways
But the people of Westerham
   Pester 'em.

The people at Barming
   Are charming
But the people at Shoreham
   Ignore 'em.

The people at Seal
   Are genteel
But the people at Malling
   Appalling.

The people of Loose
   Are some use
But the people of Brasted
   Are wasted.

FRUIT THOUGHT

An apple a day
Keeps the doctor away
If I eat nine or ten
What will the doctor do then?

Mysterious Things

AIR ON AN ESCALATOR

Gallop up the instant stair
running is as good as flying
past the ads for underwear
things you'd never dream of buying
what's that echo of despair?
that's the escalator sighing

past the ads for underwear
things you'd never dream of buying
diving belles with floating hair
take us with you! sadly crying
what's that echo of despair?
that's the escalator sighing

diving belles with floating hair
take us with you! sadly crying
no we couldn't, wouldn't dare
sorry dears, it's no use trying
what's that echo of despair?
that's the escalator sighing

no we couldn't, wouldn't dare
sorry dears, it's no use trying
gallop up the instant stair
running is as good as flying
what's that echo of despair?
that's the escalator sighing

DOWN BELOW

There's a deep secret place, dark in the hold of this ship
A fine, private place, if one could get down there and hide
A whole crossword puzzle of ladder and corridor lies
Between that world and the white decks, the smooth wide
Expanse of holystone and elbowgrace and pride.

Could one get down there; but that's quite out of the question
I'll tell you why: clambering down to the door
Through those hot, narrow regions, you notice more and
   more strongly
A green growing odour seeping up through the floor
And the damp solid breath of mould, savagely pure.

That door can't be opened; it's blocked tight shut inside
Crammed against earth and greenery, all intertwined—
Roses, perhaps? The ship is listing, but skipper,
Though the hold should be cleared, is afraid of what
   we'd find,
He believes there's stowaways down there—but, good lord,
   what kind?

π IN THE SKY

Who'll solve my problem? asks the moon
   Moving across the sky
Who'll calculate my radius
   And multiply by π?

The shining flood of light I pour
   By half a world is shared
And yet this area, figured out
   Is merely πr^2

The laws of π all circles must
   Unquestioning obey
Yet lovely as a lily, I
   Float heedless on my way

My proud contention this, which once
   The ancient Romans held:
Luna se movet—briefly put
   The moon is self-propelled.

Night's Queen I trace a silvery
   Circumference of sky
And share my cold and regal sway
   With nobody but π.

MAN AND OWL

He has trained the owl to wake him
just before it goes off to sleep
and he in his turn rouses the sleeping owl
before he starts counting sheep
and the owl lullabies him into darkness
with its wit and its woo
then owl and man snore companionably together
till the first cocks crow
only the owl's great yellow eyes are wide open
the man's like closed cupboards in his face
but their thoughts run parallel: the owl's on mice,
                              the man's on money
nature has organised this partnership neatly
which is not always the case

MOTORWAY REFLECTION

The wind is standing still and we are moving
we therefore have a greater way to go
but this there's little likelihood of proving

the wind erodes a barren ground engraving
Sahara on the coast of Waterloo
the wind is standing still and we are moving

the act of being loved outgraces loving
the target's arc must circumscribe the bow
but this there's little likelihood of proving

the wind is blind to winter leaves unweaving
but we, aware, must care for what we do
the wind is standing still and we are moving

at the wind's door we therefore lay our grieving
reaped by the wind so much of what we sow
but this there's little likelihood of proving

oh we must mourn the lonely wind surviving
becalmed in nowhere; nowhere else to blow
the wind is standing still and we are moving
but this there's little likelihood of proving

AS GOOD AS A FEAST?

Waiting in this great mansion, tom tiddler's ground
Where some kind of conference was being held
Waiting for the time when I would have to play a part
I wandered upstairs: two great flights divided like a river
Around a heartshaped hollow, to the upper storey
Where from Venetian chandeliers, old, beautiful, but
   damaged,
Fine gold dust was all the time falling, falling; I stood
   beneath one
And the gold dust fell in a bright cloud on to my hair, into
   my eyes
Standing there I thought as follows:
      Enough butter to wrap round a red-hot poker
      Enough salt to taste of the sea
      Enough water to drown memory
      Enough bricks to build half a pyramid
      Enough air to contain it
      Enough earth for a grave . . .
At this point the stinging gold in my eyes woke me.

Will anybody who can interpret these words please
Write to Box X 22.

CHARTER FLIGHT

What did the captain say when you took him a cup of tea?
He said there were hundreds of icebergs as far as the eye
  could see
And the sound of seals barking was a most forlorn and
  doleful cry
In all that ice. And the northern lights, red and green, were
  like a fire opal in the sky.

Everything in that northern world was hard and bright, he
  said,
It was like flying over a jewelled crown on someone's head
The stars flashing sharper than headlights above, while,
  low and dim
The midnight sun shone, a great smoky ruby on the world's
  rim.

The captain comes back to the airport all dislocated, and
  wanders about
The whole day in a daze, instead of sensibly going to bed
It's a good thing his route is over the north pole, not the
  south
Or as likely as not he'd pass the time between trips just
  standing on his head.

THE PUNISHMENT

I took a shell. I shouldn't have. It lay
bright, flecked, below the water of the bay;
someone still *lived* inside its curves, a person,
to leave it in the sun was bad as arson:

I left it in the sun.
                     And, when it died,
emptied the shell of what had been inside.

Bread bakes to toast, left lying in that sun
but heat can't bake out guilt for what was done.

Cleared of its inmate, sterile, yet the shell
sent out, implacably, a deadly smell
a fierce, putrescent smell of living death
of rancid sea, of horrors underneath.

The smell pursued, despite all exorcism
it wound its way through night and day like poison
no scouring powder nor detergent foam
could drive that stinking phantom from its home
air-freshener nor fly-spray, polish, none—
it breathed out rancour, it would *not* be gone.

Grown frantic for a breath of taintless air
I stuffed the orifice with newspaper . . .

here it lies, stoppered, sulking, waiting: lever
the paper out, the smell comes fierce as ever

I lay the shell against my hearkening ear
rattle of blood sounds loud as rifle fire
but never yet the murmur of the tide
nor ever will; the angry ghost inside
holds the sea prisoner in my stolen shell
emits instead the immitigable *smell*.

What power will purge? I cannot keep my crime
forever plugged with pages torn from *Time*?

DANGEROUS JOURNEY

Who's that great vandal of a child you carry?
How will you get him home through this rocky pass?
Already beneath his weight your arm is sagging
You long to kneel and settle him down on the grass

Above you the waterfall pounces down the hillside
In a furious zigzag to threaten his heavy head
Rivers like arrows menace from all directions
What madness made you bring him this way to bed?

Through the bridge you intended to cross huge trees have
    broken
And grass that is sharper than knives grows thick as a pall
In my opinion you'll never be home by twilight
There's not much chance you'll ever be home at all.

NIGHT LANDSCAPE

Rolling and tossing out sparkles like roses
puffing out plum-coloured smoke as it goes is
a cedarwood train
on an ebony plain
whose passenger muses or gazes or dozes

the boy on the train is guard, passenger, driver
who reads while he drives, while the train, like a diver,
soars, plunges, and swoops
describes hundreds of loops
all veiled in its vapour like Lady Godiva

the boy is the track is the train is the cedar
from which it was carved, is the book, is the reader
who turns out the light
and shoots into night
and spends all his dream playing follow-my-leader

JOHN'S SONG

It's a long walk in the dark
on the blind side of the moon
and it's a long day without water
when the river's gone
and it's hard listening to no voice
when you're all alone

so take a hundred lighted candles with you
when you walk on the moon
and quickly quickly tie a knot in the river
before the water's gone
and listen for my voice, if for no other
when you're all alone

SOCKS AND SHOCKS

Serene when the moon's in winter quarters
Smile the owners of electric garters
Given as prizes to the hundred winners
Of "Why I eat Leggatt's TV Dinners."

Honi (D.C.) *qui mal y pense*
No shame from sliding sockwear haunts
The owner of a sixty-watt electric garter
All-dry mains, with   sep. self-starter.

In every household, under the floor
Lie a thousand garters, or maybe more
Garters can vanish like morning dew
Lucky the lad who can muster two.

Electric garters, all-magnetic
Radar-activated, sympathetic
Fly together when you let them go
Like Romiet and Julio.

However far they are tossed asunder
Electric garters never wander
Never short-circuit, don't get lost
Keep your shinbones warm as toast

Send out warning signals in fogs
Repel advances of unfriendly dogs
Administer massage to a football bruise
Need no suppressors, never fuse.

Just one query: what about shocks?
No need to worry if you earth your socks!

FOOTPRINTS

Where did they start? those well-marked white
Cloud-footprints, two by two,
Moving at leisured pace across
The skylight's square of blue?

I ran outside: the trails traversed
From skyscape's rim to rim;
Abominable Skymen? Or
Two strolling Seraphim?

A smaller trail, of dogprints, turned
Meandering through the air
Diverging (on some sky-hunt?) from
The heedless, strolling pair.

Who were those strollers? Where their home?
What quarter of the sky?
Why were their footprints seen by none,
No single soul but I?

I HAVE

Possessions tie him to his grave
He cannot breathe, he cannot move
Bound by the terrible I have
He shuts himself from air and love.

By mothballs and by storage chests
His years are shortened to a span
With banks and battles and bequests
Man eats away the life of man.

But there will be no England France
No house no land no brush nor comb
No goods transmitted in advance
Between the deathbed and the tomb.

APOLLO AND DAPHNE

The love I chased has turned to laurel
    And now repels the rash embrace
Armoured in leather leaves, with branches
    Brittle and sharp and lacking grace.

In autumn, when the molten forest
    Shrieks at the gale with which it strives
She stands, smug, safe, and truly proper
    The guardian of suburban drives.

Legends

IF

Many remember the learned professor
who lived in a cave on the cliff
adopted two whitethroats (one greater, one lesser)
and rowed them around in a skiff
and was writing a book about *If* . . .

Oh, many remember this learned old person
who knew such a lot about words
whose history of *But* no review was adverse on
who took such kind care of the birds
(he fed them on currants and curds)

Oh, many remember how once in October
the wind was beginning to moan
as he rambled the foreshore, abstracted and sober,
he picked up a page that had blown
down the shingle from sources unknown:

"If Caesar had suffered from chronic bronchitis
if hopes may be liars (it said),
if sunrise no longer to follow the night is
if feathers were heavy as lead
if yellow and orange made red—"

Oh, many recall how his tears on that paper
like cataracts started to pour
how he ran to his skiff and, through spray, foam, and vapour,
rowed swiftly away from the shore
since then we have seen him no more . . .

But many believe that our learned old oracle
today is residing in bliss
that his goal was a land, when he left in his coracle,
where the words are inventions of *his*—
oh, many are certain of this

On a shore where the adverbs are scattered like amber
our gentle old genius now strays
over pronouns like pearls, over nouns he can clamber
knee-deep, to the end of his days
where the adjectives peacefully graze . . .

Oh, many remember the learned professor
who lived in a cage with two birds
(a couple of whitethroats, one greater, one lesser)
and thought all the time about words
and thought all the time about words . . .

BAD DREAM

This boy
got caught in his own dream
it was a dream about moss
hanging from branches
and about water
growing upwards like a tree
it was a dream about cats
like black holes in the wall
about birds in reverse
about time like a knife blade
bending sideways
it was a bad dream to get caught in
he began to scream

in this dream things were all bright and black
leaves were metal bars
a tortoiseshell moon
snapped its comb-teeth
a dragon lay waiting
under an enormous leaf

in this dream trouble was underfoot
hidden and rustling
in this dream the sun was low
sidelong and unkind
pointing a sly finger
across his mind
it was a bad dream to be caught in
he struggled to turn back

in this dream a fluttering roar overhead
sucked off his fingernails
stairs led neither up nor down
but sideways into space
in this dream motion turned inward
like a purse
and some things flickered
that should have kept still
and things that ought to move
did not
which was worse
and nothing had much of a shape
and his head was a lid
it was a bad dream to be caught in.

Did he ever escape?
I never heard that he did.

THE MAN WHO STOPPED THE BIRDS

The day the peartree started singing
The thrush's leaves began to grow
Green branches through his feathers springing
Sealed up the wells of song below.

Who did this dreadful thing? We know him.
He was a wild one; but he's gone
No one knows where; the birds would curse him
But each sits voiceless and alone.

Thanks then to him, if you go walking
By grove and hedge, the songs that flood
Come not from birds, to silence fallen
But pouring from the living wood.

THE SHADOW ON THE MAP

How do I know? Why, one afternoon
Miss Pallant (geography) all on her own
With her back to a pearl-coloured polythene moon
That peered through the chalk-dusted windowpane
Had drawn on the blackboard a large map of Spain . . .

The chalk it squeaked and the clock it ticked
Ever so peaceful and matter-of-fact
As her slender arm's shadow slipped and crept
Over Castile—when somebody stepped
Quickly behind Miss Pallant and tacked
Her shadow to Spain—what a devilish act!

Pinned like a moth by her shadow, Miss Pallant
Tore herself loose to defy her assailant
Only to find the room empty and silent!

Who could have been so invisibly violent?

No one can answer. But how can she feel
With never a shadow to follow her trail
Never a shadow to follow at heel
Whether the sunlight be brilliant or pale.

And still hangs her shadow, as proof of my tale
Dusty and wan, on the map of Castile!

HE'D JUST COME FROM THE CHURCHYARD

Two people asked
standing on the pier
would you mind—we're honeymooning—
taking our picture here?
Sorry, can't, I'm blind—
and edged past them;
it wasn't true
had they but known
she was Medusa; if she'd looked at them through the
    viewfinder
they'd have been turned to stone.

Walking backwards the boy
signalled for a lift
as if he were
conducting an orchestra of rain
car didn't stop
little did he know
once those teeth were in his neck
his mother would never have made pie for him again.

Truck driver said
can you tell me the way to Church Street
somewhere near, there's a lot of lilacs
and a gold ball on the spire
sorry, friend, I'm a stranger here myself
twirling the lilac flower behind his back
it was a lie
he'd just come from the churchyard
what he'd been doing, better not inquire.

IN THE OLD HOUSE
(*A true story*)

House silent
grandchildren put to bed
she was drinking
a glass of sherry
among strewn building blocks
and woolly animals
by the sitting-room fire
when on the stairs she heard
patter of feet.

"Go back to bed!" she called
no answer
but the feet came on downstairs.

So, crossly,
out into the hall
there he came:
down the stairs
no grandchild of hers—
about six
nightshirt
half asleep
clutching his blanket
sucking his thumb

didn't say anything, went on
straight past her across the hall
into the kitchen, but when she followed
he was gone
never seen before or since.

Was it the presence of other children in the old house
that called him so briefly
from his deep
deep sleep?

PALACE COOK'S TALE

The two little princesses
live in this palace
large as the whole of Birmingham
they aren't allowed to meet
except for five minutes every day
they are not allowed to play.

I take up their midmorning snack
a glass of buttermilk and a piece of hardtack.

Stick primroses through all the holes in a colander
you will have some notion
of their pretty ways;
yellowhaired they are, pale as the sky;
poor little dears, they hardly seem human
their smiles are like
thin thin slices of lemon.

I take up their teatime tray
black bread and a glass of whey.

They write each other letters
Dear Queenie, Dearest Regina
I was so happy to see you today
we smiled at each other
you borrowed my copy of *The Borrowers*
I think I heard you practising the piano
from far away.

Poor little things
when they grow up they will marry foreign kings.

ESKIMO LEGEND

In the tug of war between winter and summer
you should be careful how you take sides
it is better to stay neutral between such great forces
oh, you may light a fire of bones for the spring to come
   and warm herself
light it on the shore where she will see it
but in the autumn shut your doors
for it is then that ghosts come knocking
in the autumn gales they come knocking
fathers, grandfathers, older ones still
people who are better forgotten
under the floor you can hear them too
and sometimes a huge dog is with them.
In the tug of war between winter and summer
you should be careful how you take sides
the magician is the only one who has power over such forces
and even he has little control in these matters
he says he can catch the sun in a cat's-cradle net
made of seaweed
he says he can direct the wind with a seaweed whip
frankly I don't believe him
better in the autumn shut your door.

When my younger brother was sick, the magician
took away his soul for safekeeping
but he forgot to bring it back
my brother is still waiting, waiting for his soul
which the magician locked up in a soapstone box
it cried to him through the keyhole, it told him
when the ice was likely to melt
which way the winds were going to blow
what time the sun would rise.
One day the magician put out to sea
taking my brother's soul with him in the box, in the boat
maybe the soul grew tired of waiting?
Maybe it gave him the wrong advice?
His boat sank, he never came back
where is my brother's soul now?
My brother waited and waited
it never came back.
In the autumn, shut yourself in, pay no attention to the
   knocking
in the spring you may light a fire of bones on the shore
for Sedna to come and warm herself
but in the tug of war between winter and summer
it is better not to take sides.

THE FISHERMAN WRITES A LETTER TO
THE MERMAID

This water is so clear
my boat appears to float on air
and casts its shadow on sand
green as a mermaid's hand

the water is so still
I could carve words upon it with a quill
back-to-front sentences in bloodred ink
and watch them sink

while she, sky-gazing there below
could read, uncoiling slow
like trails of apple-peel
downward beneath my keel:

dear distant friend
even a ray of light must bend
to glide from me to you
so how may words pierce through?

yet think it not too hard
our lives are laid apart
this gulf is hardly greater than
that between man and man

(less, truly, for his tear
sinks, and will touch her there
sharp as a barb among the submarine waves
tears are the element in which she lives)

dear distant friend
if you should chance to find
the heart I lost one green mid-ocean day
please put it by

please keep it for me shelled in pearl
some seaborne while
and do not doubt, your friend
will come to claim it in the end

THE BOY WITH A WOLF'S FOOT

The boy with a wolf's foot
runs through the streets howling
crying help me, do something
about this pain at the base of my spine
which has crept down into my toes
how can I kick a football
ride a bicycle
with a condition like mine
oh help me, but the people
shut their windows
stuff red cottonwool up their chimneys
black treacle in the keyholes
and train their eyes on electric rabbits
not to see him
they set up two government commissions to study him

one at the north pole
one at the south
two government commissions are studying his problems
and will report in five years' time.
The boy with a wolf's foot
risking hydrophobia
weeps tears of brine
which flow under their gates and
water their crocuses
oh those salty crocuses will be
bitter as lime
the boy with a wolf's foot
carries his schoolbag to the desert
after a picnic of tears and cod's roe, plants his flag
and waits for a sign
meanwhile the old black-coated bellringers
head down like ants on business
backwards like diesel engines
doggedly mumbling, climb
into the bell tower
lost in a cloud of charcoal
they ring their tocsin
but a venomous wind
carries the notes westward
and the boy with a wolf's foot
will not hear their chime.

RETURN TO NOWHERE

Into the station
at Hampton Wick
old lady steps:
black coat, white stick
cotton apron
with a flowery pattern
hat like a cushion
someone sat on

cool and silent
summer gloom
nobody else
in the waiting room
trees at the window
green and dark
nobody there
but the booking clerk

rapped on the counter
said, "Young man
round trip to nowhere
quick as you can!"
(Down train signalled
up train gone
no bird twittered
no sun shone)

clerk woke yawning
sneezed, atishoo,
"Round trips to nowhere
we don't issue."
Sniffed, "In that case
if you're able,
single to nowhere
and a new timetable."

"Single, a shilling,
timetable, two,
ten bob, seven bob,
thanking *you*."

Train came whispering
down the track
empty carriage
stick in rack
door slams briskly
off goes train
never, anywhere
seen again.

FABLE

Pity the girl with crystal hair
each dazzling strand
is bright as an icicle
but how can she run
how can she bicycle
how can she lean on the back of her chair?
should she stoop to pull up a sock
her pigtails clang like a chiming clock
how can she skip
how can she sleep?
her plight is enough to make you weep.

She stood in front of his house, she cried
Hey you old wizard? are you inside?
skipped up and down
on impudent feet
mocking and bold in the cobbled street
Hey, you old wizard! How do you do?
I'm not in the least
afraid of *you*!

Thumbed her nose and turned to run
flipped her ponytail
laughing and reckless—
all of a sudden
it shone like a necklace
blazed like a blade in the setting sun!
what'll she do?
where can she go?
spiteful magician, to treat her so!

Pity the girl with crystal hair
each dazzling strand
is beautiful, yes
but oh what a care,
what a distress
often a friend
snaps off a tress
what'll she do when her head is bare?
tap the magician's windowpane
humble and sorry
thin with the worry
beg him to take off the spell again.

53

People

GRANDFATHER

Each year, as spring returns
our house is haunted by the ghosts of ferns.

One day at breakfast Grandpa drank his cocoa
and said, "Goodbye, I'm off to Orinoco,"
packed up his bag, and went . . .
Each following year he sent
such picture postcards! One
showed us the Mexican horses of the sun
peaks of the Andes next
wind-fretted, needle-sharp, and earthquake-vexed
next year, from Chuguchak
Grandpa in blizzard, riding on a yak
next year, from Tirunel
a temple marked with cross: "This is my cell."
And every spring arrived
ferns, with a note, "Please plant"; not one survived
though potted out with care
they pined and dwindled in our civilised air.
At Resht, he died. Granny, just then enmeshed
in knitting wool, snapped, "Let him stay at Resht!"

Grandpa, goodbye! But still
the shadows of your ferns, on shelf and sill
scatter the air with flocks of ghostly spores . . .
Aunt Alice should have tried them out of doors.

THE SKIN SPINNERS

Poets, clustered like spiders, sing
shrilly of the gadfly's wing
and make of air and dust and flesh
a subtle and a silver mesh,
study the seasons and the trends
times, fashions, tides, for their own ends;
all is foretold, all comes to pass
spun, spinning, in a web of glass;
brooding above the throng of flies
they watch with penetrating eyes
and turn the living and the dead
impartially to daily bread.

THE BOG PEOPLE

They were, they were so happy
walking hand in hand
that, they remember
that, they understand

sitting by the river
strolling in the town
time caught and passed them
the slow tide went down

now they fold forever
leather hands and feet
the victim, the lover
pickling in the peat

bones, like a rucksack
she wears at her back
her leather heart within them
tucked in the pack

say she died grieving
as some people do
essence of her trouble
lies in there too

lifesize in leather
by her lover's side
there she lies resting
just as she died

ah, cover up her features
of perdurable hide
misfortune's mummy
the bog-man's bride

THE DRIVER

The reins, looped lightly round his aged knuckles
Stretch into darkness
The horses, somewhere out of sight
Trot into night

What does he look ahead to? Vacancy
Listen to? Silence
The roadside's lost in mist
His only light is in the past

Behind him, like a traveller's trunk
His life, packed tight with treasures and with junk
Where is he taking it? He does not know
But he has not far to go

MY BROTHER'S DREAM

Mother why have you brought me here, oh, where is Father?
    Cries the boy, alarmed at the gloom
And the urns and caskets of the undertaker's parlour
    I want to go home!

Wait patiently, dearest, but a little minute
    —Says Mother, cossetting, admonishing, and mild
Just see the lovely box with Papa's head in it,
    See, see, my precious child!

And, to the undertaker (sympathetic
    At the child's not unnatural fright)
She says, There, poor dear, I knew it would upset him
    Besides his being out so late at night.

Calling for Myrtle and Daphne, the child, in tears
    Turns from the mummy head and flees
—Thinking they are girls who will kiss away his fears—
    But, alas, they are trees.

MY FATHER REMEMBERS

My father remembers
the streetcar that ran round the town of Savannah
under magnolias and mockingbirds
it ran its happy way
past live-oaks and palmettoes
(once two bears climbed up one of the live-oaks and
  refused to come down
that was a great day)
my father remembers
how when the streetcar one time came clanking off its track
his father
who must have been a strong man
lifted it up and put it back
he remembers eating sugarcane, sitting on the kerb
and spitting the pith on to the sidewalk
which was all made of brick set in a herringbone pattern
under Spanish moss dangling like the beard of time.

My father remembers
looking out of the window, seeing a man murdered
in front of the fire station by the streetcar track
by the great firebell
nobody seemed to care

The streetcar went running
past marble steps and wrought-iron railings
all round the town of Savannah
across the marshes to the south
and there, for some reason,
it swooped up on to a viaduct and went soaring along
in mid air
looking out over the marshes
why did the streetcar do that?
there seemed no reason for it

No one remembers the viaduct
no one apart from my father
maybe it was for him alone, when he was a boy
just for the fun of it
that the streetcar flew up into the air and went swinging along
high over the marshes
and the town of Savannah?

THE SMILE

My grandmother, I've discovered
Keeps a smile in her bedside cupboard
Soft in the morning you hear her say
"Tom? Do I feel like smiling today?"

And Tom (Grandfather, that is; he died
Twenty years back, at Whitsuntide)
Tom says, "Yes, love!" from out of the sky
"Yes, love! You're feeling as perky as pie."

So Granny she reaches out from bed
And snaps the elastic over her head . . .

At night she takes off the shawl Ma made
And her button boots and her hearing-aid
And only then when she's all undressed
Does she take the smile off and let it rest.

OUTING

Every time I visit a strange town
I take my mother with me

I can feel her seeing through my eyes
gazing at shopwindows, longing to buy a book, a toy, a
    heavy glass jug
"Shall we go and look at the cathedral?" she says
I can hear her listening to two old ladies by the post office
"That one says local, that one says all other places"
"I can read, can't I? I was just taking me time. I can have a
    look, can't I?"

I can feel her wanting to comfort some crying child
wanting to get into conversation with some glum-looking man
and cheer him up
"Do let's go down that dear little street and see where it
    goes," she says
as often as not
it is a cul-de-sac, ending in a builder's yard
which only amuses her
I can feel her hoping there will be beautiful strange things in
    the shops

and a river with bridges and somebody playing the organ
in the cathedral
I can feel this active love
she had of doing and seeing
going and being
work in me like yeast as I walk new streets
not memory but an overlap
from her life to mine; not memory; you do not remember
what is still happening
I do not begin where she ended, for she has not ended

every time I visit a strange town and walk strange streets
I take her with me

Ballads

THE BALLAD OF NEWINGTON GREEN

There was a young lady of Newington Green
Had the luck to be loved by a sewing machine
Its foot was so slender, its eye was so bright
It sewed so obligingly, morning or night
On nylon or seersucker, silk or sateen
Her sturdy, reliable Singer machine!

It made her a shirt, and a shift, and a shawl
Pants, petticoat, poncho, pyjamas, and all
A jacket, a jerkin, a veil, and a vest
For every affair she was perfectly dressed
A coat and some curtains, a pink crinoline
Were made by her hard-working Singer machine.

It hemmed and it quilted, it ran and it felled
At tucks and at pleats and at darts it excelled
If she gave it some smocking or basting or shirring
It worked with a will and was often heard purring
How I love you! she cried, oh my darling machine
My shapely sweet Singer of Newington Green.

She went to a dance in the Holloway Road
In the pink crinoline that her Singer had sewed
Fell in love as she sipped on a Coke at the bar
With the fellow who played the electric guitar
Her love was returned; he exclaimed, My princess
We'll be married next week; all you need is a dress.

Come help me, my Singer, here's satin and lace
For I'm to be married in seven days' space
Come make me a wedding dress pleated and frilled
My swift shapely Singer, so sturdy and skilled.
The Singer obliged, but it sighed in between
Every stitch that it sewed, poor heartbroken machine.

The wedding was over, the couple were gone
The heartbroken Singer was left all alone
In grief and despair it stood sighing and sobbing
Tears ran down its needle and into its bobbin
Till rust had demolished that lovelorn machine
The sorrowful Singer of Newington Green.

LOOK OUT FOR THE PLATFORM

Look out for the platform
   Before you alight
For if by mischance
   You stepped into the night
On the side of the train
   That's away from the station
You might not arrive at
   Your true destination.

On *this* side's a platform
   But who can be sure
Where you'd be if you chanced
   To step out by *that* door?
On this side lights, luggage,
   The name of some place
On the other side, nothing
   But darkness and space.

On this side is Reading—
   Or Tooting—or Epping—
But you might on the other
   Side find yourself stepping
Right into a land
   Where the moon shines all day
Where horses have fins
   And the sharks live on hay—

Where you watch out at night
  For the terrible whale
Who cames galloping after you
  Threshing his tail—
Where the sirens sing ballads
  And play on guitars
Where apples and walnuts
  Shine brighter than stars.

So look for the platform
  Before you alight
For if by mischance
  You step into the night
By the door that would lead you
  Straight on to the track
It's a thousand to one
  You would never come back.

71

NEW YORK SEWERS

They say the drains of New York town
    Are full of alligators
Their numbers only to be reckoned
    By countless calculators
Their origin the tourists, home
    From southern holidays
Who bring as happy souvenirs
    The caymans from the cays

It's hard to spurn a cayman's sweet
    Ingratiating smile
(A cayman I should mention is
    A kind of crocodile)
They bring the infant muggers home
    And keep them in the tub
And feed them prawns and jellied eels
    And other lovely grub.

A cayman in the bath may be
    At first a source of pride
But presently may prove to have
    Its inconvenient side
When old Aunt Rose, about to wash
    Is startled by the sight
Of saurian smiles beside the soap
    She may fall dead of fright

And that is why the plug is pulled
  On infant crocodiles
Who all go whirling down the waste
  Despite their winning wiles
And why the drains of New York town
  Are full of lashing tails
And toothy snouts and bulging eyes
  And scrawny snouts and scales.

I'm glad I'm not a sewerman
  In New York's underground
And what is more, I wouldn't be
  For twenty thousand pound.

CHERRYSTONES

Cherries upon a plate, Eliza Jane?
She counts them anxiously and shakes her head
—*Tinker and tailor, beggarman again.*

Flyer, sky-witted, who may seek in vain,
Grown old, those windy roads he used to tread?
—*Cherries upon a plate, Eliza Jane?*

Fisher who skims above the salty main
Or silent sinks below it, lapped in lead?
—*Tinker and tailor, beggarman again.*

Baker by bun-warm oven, safe and sane,
Shaping his lumpish life to loaves of bread?
—*Cherries upon a plate, Eliza Jane?*

Miner? The whole wide world's his counterpane
Digger of dark, he makes the rock his bed.
—*Tinker and tailor, beggarman again.*

What gleaming secrets do these stones contain?
She counts them anxiously and shakes her head.
Cherries upon a plate, Eliza Jane?
—*Tinker and tailor, beggarman again.*

SOCKS FOR THE SIRENS

Oh what are they a-doing of, the sirens on the rocks?
A-nodding and a-gossiping and knitting winter socks
In saucy stripes and gaudy checks and polka dots and plaids
—When not engaged in singing songs to simple sailor lads

>Yo ho, me lads, and so, me lads, you may bet your
>   monthly money
>It's purl and plain upon the main that keeps the sirens
>   sunny.

Oh what are they a-doing of, the mermaids in the grottoes?
A-giving cracker parties and a-reading out the mottoes?
But no, they crochet winter vests to keep them from the cold
And play upon their lutes and flutes and triangles of gold.

>Yo ho, me lads, and so, me lads, attend this wisdom
>   weighty
>It's crochet on the ocean blue that keeps the mermaids
>   matey.

And what about the Loreleis a-sitting by the streams
Enticing with their lullabies young oarsmen into dreams?
When not engaged in lullabies they weave warm underwear
To keep them from the clammy rocks and chilly winter air.

>Yo ho, me lads, and so, me lads, you'll take, if you are
>   wise
>Some shuttles and some wool to please the lovely
>   Loreleis.

CHANGE OF WIND

Music is snobbish too, alack! there are social classes
Even in Lydia, even on the green slopes of Parnassus
Some instruments are better tone than others, some are low
Strings are superior to brass and woodwind, did you know?
Strings are highclass, but wind-players are an inferior set
Flute, oboe, trumpet, piccolo, horn, bassoon, and clarinet.

All this arose when night music was a commercial affair
You dined inside and the players serenaded in the open air
Except those instruments affected by damp such as strings
    or tambour
Which were therefore privileged to come into the supper
    chamber
But the wind players stood outside in the courtyard getting
    wet:
Flute, oboe, trumpet, piccolo, horn, bassoon, and clarinet.

Mozart changed all that; some of his best friends played
    the oboe
(Which in those days was a low occupation, little better
    than being a hobo)
He wrote quartets for them, cassations, concerti, and
    serenades,
Sinfonie concertante and divertimenti in positive
    cascades

He lavished these musical offerings on them without stint
Despite the risk that no publisher would put such vulgar
    stuff into print
Consideration like this had never been shown to them yet:
Flute, oboe, trumpet, piccolo, horn, bassoon, and clarinet.

Having a special fondness for clarinets, Mozart gladdened
    their hearts
By going on to write piano concerti in which he gave them
    marvellous parts
Almost equal to that of the soloist, an unheard-of thing
    to do!
And then his friend Beethoven took hold of the notion and
    did it too
So the wind-players, hitherto such tag, rag, and bobtail
At last began to rise higher in the orchestral scale.
No longer would they have to stand outside in the dark
    and wet
Flute, oboe, trumpet, piccolo, horn, bassoon, and clarinet.

NATE'S SONG

Oh blue blows the lilac and green grows the corn
And the isle of Nantucket is where I was born
Sweet isle of Nantucket! where the grapes are so red
And the light flashes nightly on Sankety Head.

Off Sankety Headland a whale is residing
As rosy as sunrise, as round as a whiting
Neither twister nor hurricane, tempest nor gale
Will chase from Nantucket its sociable whale.

Oh lucky Nantucket, oh fortunate land
Your natives dance daily quadrilles on the strand
And carpets of oystershells nightly are spread
'Twixt Polpis and Sconset and Sankety Head.

A shepherd I'll be and daylong will I rove
A-following my lambkins in meadow and grove
In the isle of Nantucket I'll finish my days
A-following my lambkins and a-watching them graze

Sweet whale of Nantucket, so pink and so nice
As rosy and round as a strawberry ice
By Providence blest to our shores you were led
Long, long may you gambol off Sankety Head!

INDEX OF FIRST LINES

ABOUT THE AUTHOR

The daughter of the poet Conrad Aiken and the sister of two professional writers, JOAN AIKEN began writing at the age of five because, as she says, "Writing is just the family trade."

Ms. Aiken wrote about two thirds of the poems in this volume in the last ten years, "most of the rest in the previous ten years, two in the forties, and two in the thirties. Which doesn't mean," she says, "that I write more poetry now—in the thirties and forties I wrote practically *nothing but* poetry, and it was terrible. I'm more selective nowadays. And poetry comes in spells, like weather; sometimes there will be months of drought, then two or three good spells together. Outside circumstances are more important to me now—before I was twenty I wrote poems anywhere, in class, on buses, in the bath, especially when I was hungry—now I need to be alone for long spells, or they don't work out."

Joan Aiken has had published nearly thirty books for adults and children alike. *The Mooncusser's Daughter: A Play for Children,* and *Midnight Is a Place,* a novel, were recently published by Viking. She lives in Sussex, England, and in New York City.

ABOUT THE ARTIST

KEN RINCIARI was born in the Bronx and lives in New York City. His work has appeared in many leading magazines, including *The New York Times Book Review, Natural History,* and *Smithsonian.* He works best at night.

ABOUT THIS BOOK

The text type used in *The Skin Spinners* is Weiss Linotype and the display is Caslon Openface. The art work was done by pen and shot as line. Printed by offset, the book is bound in cloth and paper over boards.